Purple Passion Majesty

WRITTEN BY
BRENDA G. MOORE

CROOKED TREE
STORIES

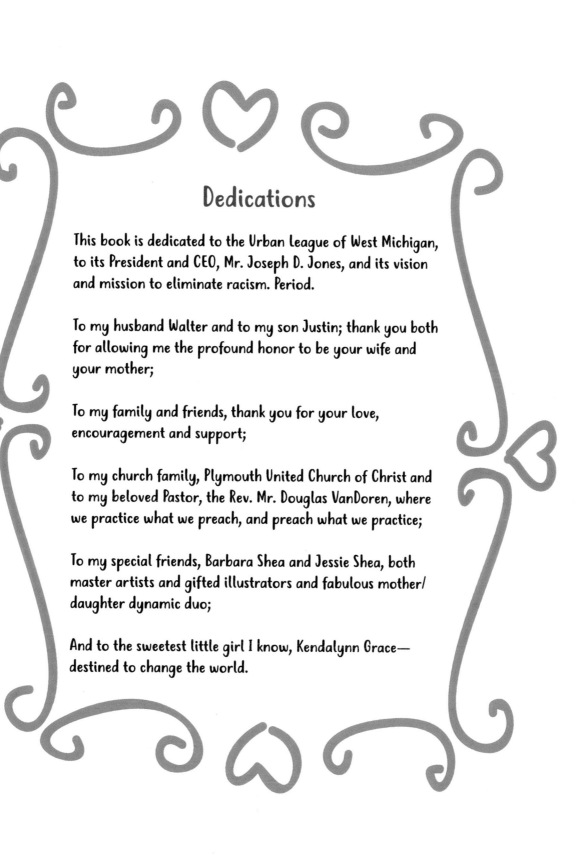

Dedications

This book is dedicated to the Urban League of West Michigan, to its President and CEO, Mr. Joseph D. Jones, and its vision and mission to eliminate racism. Period.

To my husband Walter and to my son Justin; thank you both for allowing me the profound honor to be your wife and your mother;

To my family and friends, thank you for your love, encouragement and support;

To my church family, Plymouth United Church of Christ and to my beloved Pastor, the Rev. Mr. Douglas VanDoren, where we practice what we preach, and preach what we practice;

To my special friends, Barbara Shea and Jessie Shea, both master artists and gifted illustrators and fabulous mother/daughter dynamic duo;

And to the sweetest little girl I know, Kendalynn Grace— destined to change the world.

Never doubt that a small group of thoughtful committed citizens can change the world; indeed, it's the only thing that ever has.

—Margaret Mead

Once upon a time in the kingdom of More, two lands existed like never before.
A fresh water lake separated the two; on one side was red, the other side blue.
In the kingdom of More there was frankly, well—less. Less sun, less fun, it was a complete hot mess.

The two groups of people who lived in More, thought more highly of themselves than ever before. Identifying scarves adorned their heads; the ones to the left were the ones who wore red. Blue was the color that was worn on the right; both groups wore their scarves during the day and at night.

In the land of red, there was so much to dread.
The food, the clothes, even the grass was dead.
Food was limited to just a few things, tomatoes in summer and apples in spring.

Blue land was no better, it was dark and cloudy. People felt sad one minute but the next could be rowdy. The land of blue had limited food too, only blueberries, blue corn, and blue cheese, whew! The clothes and environment were just as bad, in the land of blue, it was all so sad.

The people of More, all experienced less, because of distrust, dishonor and other foolishness. Folks on the red side believed they were superior, while folks on the blue side thought red were inferior. Sadness and depression ruled both sides of the lake; the arguing and bickering led to pain and heartache. The people were stubborn, too blind to see, that they needed each other to achieve their destiny.

If only they could see the need to honor and embrace; each other's differences face-to-face. But the people refused to seek each other's advice, guided by hatred and other things not nice. So the suffering continued by day and by night, for the red on the left and blue on the right.

"We'll have nothing to do with them," said each group about the other.
"We won't like them, respect them, or be nice to one another!"

With hate in their hearts and meanness in their eyes, they vowed to be separate and continue to despise.

Refusing to speak when seen across the lake, believing the worst things about each other causing more heartache.

Except for two little girls—one from the left and another from the right, who could only talk to each other across the lake at night.

The girl from the left was named Kendalynn, and she just wanted the relationships to mend. The girl on the right felt the same way too; her name was Grace, and she was tired of the fighting, too. Both girls were lovely, smart and cute; they were healthy and strong and funny to boot.

Every day, Grace asked if she could play, with the little girl Kendalynn who lived across the way. From morning until night Kendalynn asked too, for permission to play with Grace, it was nothing new. The answer came back always the same; from both of their mothers who loudly proclaimed, "You cannot ever, ever play with any little girl from across that way!"

"I don't understand," said Grace shaking her head. "Why can't I? Is it because she is red?" "Is she so different from me?" asked Grace.

"No my dear," said her mother, "it's just race."

"I don't understand," Grace went on to say, "Why would we allow race to stand in our way?"

"Because it's what we believe, it's what we've been taught; this is not our battle and it can't be fought." "But we can and we must!" Grace said, "Don't you see? Our way of living equals inequality."

"It's the law," said her mother, "the law of the land."

"Who created this law?" Grace asked, "Was it merely a man?"

"We'll ask the elders, they'll know what to do." So Grace and Kendalynn started asking a few.

As they stood before the elders, both girls began debating, the need for such laws, it was very frustrating! The elders listened carefully and asked questions, too. Kendalynn and Grace just hoped that they knew, that treating others differently was the wrong thing to do.

Respecting the elders for their knowledge, experience, and wisdom; both girls continued their pleas for a new, improved system. Where everyone is welcomed, honored and included; not separated, *othered*, avoided, or unsuited.

But the elders were committed to continuing to affirm, their traditional beliefs and practices no matter what they had learned. All the elders voted "no" from the left to the right, and for Kendalynn and Grace it was a very sad night.

So the girls began praying for a land where they could be free; a land of respect, honor, and unity.

So they made a plan to connect at midnight. Kendalynn and Grace were ready to take flight.

"I'm excited to start over in a brand new land," said Kendalynn as she waved her little hand.

"I agree," said Grace, "I love the color blue; but I'd like to know more about being red, too." So the two girls walked the shore of the lake, with a plan to reach the other by daybreak.

But during the night, when their moms checked their beds; they saw neither girl and were quite filled with dread. When they found the girls missing they sounded alarms: uptown, downtown, in the city, and on the farms. People on the left and the right, the blue and the red, joined together that night and forged straight ahead.

They put aside their differences and worked through the night, walking and talking
and cooperating, that's right! Comforting each other, with hope and caring; there
was no anger, hatred, disrespect, or swearing. Hand-in-hand, arm-in-arm, they
marched through the night; the red and blue unity was a wonderful sight. Displaying
love and honor one to another, no longer enemies, but sisters and brothers.

When to their relief, both girls were in sight; their fathers scooped them up and hugged them so tight.

"We were so worried!" said the mothers to the girls. "What were you thinking, what in the world?"

"We want to be free," said the girls to the crowd. "We don't want to live where hatred is allowed."

They tried as best they could to hold each other tight, but their fathers pulled the girls apart and separated them that night.

"We cannot go back to the way that it was!" both the girls cried.

"But it's what we've been taught," said the crowd, "and believe deep inside."

"But parents and neighbors," said Grace, "don't you see? That's just wrong thinking and it just cannot be!"

Kendalynn shouted, "Why should color cause us to divide? Instead we should focus on what is inside."

The girls began to cry and held more tightly to each other, but were finally pulled apart by their fathers and some others. Back to being separate, one red, the other blue; *Would it always be this way?* Kendalynn and Grace wondered, too.

The crowds were ashamed of their behavior thus far, but lacked the courage to change and treat others on par. So red scarves went left, blues scarves went right; but something miraculous happened that night. Two brave little girls, made a big, bold move; it was genius, clever, and oh so smooth! Quick as a wink and with all their might, the girls tied their scarves together that night.

At that very moment something magical occurred, the sky lit up brightly and birds were stirred. A mighty wind appeared and began to encircle, and to everyone's surprise the scarves all turned purple!

"Oh my, oh my," roared the voices from the crowd; look at all the possibilities that purple has allowed! Both inside and outside the people could see, just how much better their lives could be.

Purple fruits and vegetables danced in the sky, there was eggplant, cabbage, even potatoes, oh my! Plums, berries, and purple beets, too; purple onions, purple grapes, purple tomatoes, who knew? Purple flowers sprouted up out of the ground; violets, orchids, and lilacs all around. Purple shoes, purple socks; purple doors and purple locks; purple pants, and purple smocks, purple birds, and peacocks.

The magic of purple was all that it took, to make the people of More take an inside look. In their hearts and minds that were hardened by hate, they decided to start loving instead on that date. All the people were happy and finally agreed, that hating one another was silly indeed!

Combining red and blue created the color purple; the people rejoiced and held hands in a circle. Purple symbolizes royalty, and blue means trust; red stands for passion, and love is a must. More colors of the rainbow appeared in their sight, bringing energy and power to everyone that night.

"We are all connected on the journey of life; it's much too precious to allow hatred and strife."

"We can do better," they shouted, "we can make real change; real talk, a new walk, there's no shame in our game!" To their surprise in the midst of their sharing, appeared a bridge over the lake because the people were caring. No longer separated, they could finally be free, to play and visit one another in true harmony.

So the people of More no longer had less, for the joy in their hearts brought out their very best.

Joining together, they each experienced more; more joy, more love, and more happiness than before.

Thanks to two little girls who didn't settle for less; they walked hand-in-hand and cried, "To all be blessed!"

Be beautiful, be wonderful, be kind and be free; treat all people with respect, love, and dignity. And when you see something purple, I hope you agree in the miracle of purple passion majesty!

A Life That Matters

- Unknown

Ready or not, some day it will all come to an end.
There will be no more sunrises, no minutes, hours, days.
All the things you collected, whether treasured or forgotten,
will pass to someone else.
Your wealth, fame and temporal power will shrivel to irrelevance.
It will not matter what you owned or what you were owed.
Your grudges, resentments, frustrations, and jealousies will finally disappear.
So, too, your hopes, ambitions, plans, and to-do lists will expire.
The wins and losses that once seemed so important will fade away.
It won't matter where you came from, or on what side of the tracks you lived.
At the end, whether you were beautiful or brilliant, male or female,
even your skin color won't matter.

So what will matter? How will the value of your days be measured?
What will matter is not what you bought, but what you built;
not what you got, but what you gave.
What will matter is not your success, but your significance.
What will matter is not what you learned, but what you taught.
What will matter is every act of integrity, compassion,
courage or sacrifice that enriched, empowered or encouraged others.
What will matter is not your competence, but your character.
What will matter is not how many people you knew, but how many
will feel a lasting loss when you're gone.
What will matter is not your memories, but the memories
that live in those who loved you.
Living a life that matters doesn't happen by accident.
It's not a matter of circumstance but of choice.
Choose to live a life that matters.

Made in the USA
Las Vegas, NV
02 June 2022

49678023R00021